FLYING LIKE FLITTERMOUSE

Jan Fearnley

For Leo,
with love
J.F.

First published in Great Britain 2013
by Egmont UK Limited
The Yellow Building, 1 Nicholas Road, London W11 4AN

ISBN 978 1 4052 6536 2 (Paperback)
ISBN 978 1 7803 1387 0 (Ebook)

Our story began over a century ago, when
seventeen-year-old Egmont Harald Petersen
found a coin in the street. He was on his way to
buy a flyswatter, a small hand-operated printing
machine that he then set up in his tiny apartment.

The coin brought him such good luck that today
Egmont has offices in over 30 countries around
the world. And that lucky coin is still kept at the
company's head offices in Denmark.

EGMONT
We bring stories to life

Look under the blueprint!

THE Pond Children — live in The Pond, in lost shoes and handbags. They are full of mischief!

Harry's long-lost cousins — Spit and Spot

The Custard Cats live in the CUSTARD CAVES. They make sweeties!

Pilot Pete — Pilots big ships into the river.

Etsuko — Happy Hamster of loveliness. She runs the tea shop.

Olivia Otter lives in Witch's Thimble, on the riverbank. She makes SPELLS and POTIONS.

Mr. Dong teaches music.

Diddly Doll the SMUGGLER often seen SKULKING around Smugglers' Bay.

THE NORTH STAR — He'll guide you home.

Hoshi and Kishuko live in Pagoda Place.

BIG LES the Tugmaster

Merlikin Mermaid — OOOH! She's very naughty. Watch out, she's a troublemaker!

N W E S — I'm not sure who this is...

Kurt and Sylvia live on Kittiwake Island.

The Lighthouse keeper is called Ping.

Captain Brock — One of the Bay's Finest sailors! Lulu

Doris and Dan

Pauline the Platypus

Norman (Olivia's apprentice in magic)

Not very far away, there's a place where the Winding River flows into the Big Wide Sea. There are boats on the water, ships in the harbour and interesting animals all around. It's a busy place, a special place — and its name is Bottlenose Bay.

HARRY the harbour mouse — He's friends with everybody! Local hero.

Samina Songbird — A wonderful singer. Samina often gives concerts at the CUSTOMS HOUSE, with the help of her backing group, the FABULOUS Singing Shells!

KIKI KOALA runs the JOLLY TUGBOAT INN.

BOZ lives at the BOATYARD with Beryl and Boof... He's a brilliant engineer and fixer of things.

Flittermouse — mysterious stranger from faraway lands...

The River Rats — Always up for trouble! Cheeky, silly, naughty, but with hearts as big as the sky.

Captain Rosie — She's sailed all over the world.

Shelley

Bottlenose Betty — She's fintastic!

Maggie Magpie runs the CHANDLERS STORE. She can get you anything. Just don't ask where it came from!

Racey Casey — lives in an old bus at the OLD QUARRY. She likes to go FAST.

Mama Bun lives on the Leas under the OLD CEDAR TREE.

The Wind... bringer of presents... taker of things... also known as Zephyr, Mistral, Sirocco, Jaku, Bora, Cierzo.

The JAGGEDY DAGGERS! OOOh, they're BAD!!! They crunch and bash and smash up boats: BEWARE! BEWARE! BEWARE!!

Kameko sea turtle

Light-Fingered Larry — His eight arms are constantly up to mischief. Watch your stuff when he's about!

Salty Steve

THE BIG WIDE SEA

The yellow teashop belonged
to Etsuko the hamster. She was
full of kindness and made
everyone welcome.

Every day, Boz the Boatbuilder
popped in for a pot of raspberry tea
and a chat. They were best friends.

One day, a mysterious stranger flew in to town.
His name was *Flittermouse*.

Flittermouse was charming.
He flew with captivating
grace and style.

He had cheeky brown eyes.
His beautiful leathery wings
folded up neatly when he
sipped his tea.

He had ears just like her.
He had claws just like her.
He had silky fur just like her.
But *he* could fly!

Etsuko was enchanted!
"I wish I could fly," she said.
"I want to soar high in the sky
and gaze at the land far below."

"Don't be silly!" said Boz.
"Hamsters can't fly."

Then she climbed up high
and flapped her wings.
She boinged the springs
and leapt into the air,

But Etsuko was
determined. She made
herself a pair of wings

and tied bouncy springs
to her feet.

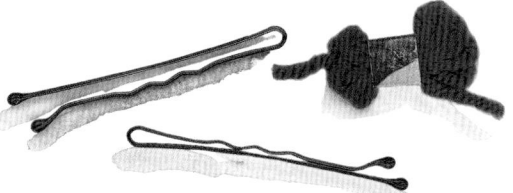

up **and** down

up!

up . . .

up . . . and

"I'm flying! Like Flittermouse!"

But then

down . . .

down . . .

down . . .

splAsh!

Boz and Boop
fished Etsuko out.

"Look where your silly ideas have got you,"
said Boz. "I told you, hamsters cannot fly."

Etsuko was sorry the plan hadn't worked.
She decided to try again.

The River Rats wanted to help. They had a
cannon that they'd found on an old shipwreck.
"We'll have you flying like a daredevil at
the circus!" they promised.

Etsuko wriggled into the barrel,

the fuse was lit and

SSSSSSSSS!!!!!

It sizzled and spat and . . .

Etsuko

shot

across the sky,

up, up, up!

"I'm flying!"

But
then

down . . .

down . . .

down . . .

splash!

Kurt Seagull plucked
Etsuko from the waves.
"I'll take you home," he said.

Nestled on Kurt's feathery back,
Etsuko gazed at the land far below.
It looked amazing.
More than ever, she longed
to fly by herself.

Back home, she saw a shadowy figure swooping gracefully through the darkening sky. It was Flittermouse.

Etsuko felt sad. Her dreams had come to nothing.

"Boz is right," she sighed. "I'm not a flittermouse, or a daredevil, or a bird. I'm just a silly little hamster."

Back at the beaver boatyard, Boz was thinking. He was fond of Etsuko, and he wanted her to be happy.

"Perhaps I've been too sensible," he said to himself. "Perhaps it *is* possible . . ."

He drew up some plans and made a list.

Next, he visited Pop Ribbet's Scrapyard and bought some supplies. He loaded up engines, wheels and pieces of metal. "What are you building?" asked Pop.

Day and night the workshop rang with all sorts of noises.

Everyone wanted to know what was happening.

"It's a secret!" said Beryl.

No peeking!

said Boop.

At last came the
time to fetch Etsuko.

"I said hamsters
can't fly," said Boz.
"I think perhaps
I was wrong."

The workshop
doors opened wide.
And there in the sunshine was a
smart red aeroplane!
It was perfect for a little hamster.

Etsuko was delighted.

She climbed into the cockpit, fired up the engine –

chocks away! – rumbled down the road,

and went

up, up, up . . .

. . . and away!

"I CAN FLY!"

cried Etsuko.

She swooped low and looped high.

She climbed and she dived.

She flew upside down!

And then Flittermouse appeared, and together they weaved through the clouds, performing amazing aerobatics in the sky.

Zoooooooom!

Thanks to Boz, Etsuko could hop in
her aeroplane and fly any time she
liked. She was very happy.

She spotted the coastline and the fairground
far below. She saw her tiny teashop.
And then she saw something very strange . . .

A dot in the sky getting bigger every second, closer and closer and closer . . .

It was *another* aeroplane.
A big blue one.

It was Boz and Beryl and Boop!

And can you guess
what they said?

"We're flying like Etsuko!"

And that is exactly what they did.
Because as anyone will tell you,
even big sensible beavers are
allowed to have silly dreams too.